QUARTERBACK SNEAK

BY JAKE MADDOX

illustrated by Sean Tiffany

text by Bob Temple

Librarian Reviewer
Chris Kreie
Media Specialist, Eden Prairie Schools, MN
MS in Information Media, St. Cloud State University, MN

Reading Consultant
Mary Evenson
Middle School Teacher, Edina Public Schools, MN
MA in Education, University of Minnesota

STONE ARCH BOOKS
Minneapolis   San Diego

Impact Books are published by Stone Arch Books,
A Capstone Imprint
151 Good Counsel Drive, P.O. Box 669
Mankato, Minnesota 56002
www.capstonepub.com

Library of Congress Cataloging-in-Publication Data
Maddox, Jake.

Quarterback Sneak / by Jake Maddox; illustrated by Sean Tiffany.
p. cm. — (Impact Books — A Jake Maddox Sports Story)
ISBN 978-1-4342-0464-6 (library binding)
ISBN 978-1-4342-0514-8 (paperback)
[1. Football—Fiction. 2. Teamwork (Sports)—Fiction.] I. Tiffany,
Sean, ill. II. Title.
PZ7.M25643Quc 2008
[Fic]—dc22
                                                    2007031256

Summary: Anton loves playing football until Malik, the talented
quarterback, starts acting strange. Instead of working with the team,
Malik is just showing off. He's hogging the ball, and the team is
starting to lose. Anton thinks it has something to do with the tall guy
in sunglasses who keeps showing up to their games. But who is he, and
why does Malik care what he thinks? Anton has to fix the problem fast,
before the quarterback ruins everything!

Art Director: Heather Kindseth
Graphic Designer: Kay Fraser

Printed in the United States of America in Stevens Point, Wisconsin.
122009
005644R

TABLE OF CONTENTS

CHAPTER 1

CALLING THE PLAY

Anton jogged out to the huddle.

His heart thumped in his chest as he ran, thinking about the situation.

The play Coach Benson had just given him called for him to get the ball.

It was the first game of the junior varsity season, and it was fourth down.

Anton's team, the Giants, only had one more chance to make a play.

The Giants were trailing 23–19. They needed to score a touchdown to win the game.

There were only six seconds left on the game clock. The ball was 20 yards from the Dolphins' goal line. Anton knew the Giants' chances weren't good.

Twenty yards. One play.

Anton liked the play the coach had called. It was 23 fake flat right.

Anton had to fake taking a handoff from his team's quarterback, Malik.

Then Anton would scoot out of the backfield to the right.

Malik would fake a long pass down the middle, and then dump the ball off to Anton on the right side.

With blockers out in front of him, Anton would use his running ability to get the rest of the way to the goal.

The Dolphins had a very big, tough defensive line, but Anton wasn't worried. He didn't do his best running up the middle anyway.

He was better on the outside when they pitched him the ball.

Out there, he had some running room. Out there, he would be able to fake out the defense.

Anton was doing well in the game so far. He had scored two of his team's touchdowns. Malik had scored the other one on a quarterback sneak.

As the Giants huddled, Anton whispered the play to Malik.

It was Malik's job as quarterback to tell the rest of the team the play their coach had called.

"Got it, Malik?" Anton asked the quarterback.

But Malik wasn't looking at him.

In fact, Malik's eyes weren't even on the field.

Malik was looking over to the sideline. Anton glanced over too. He saw that a tall, athletic man wearing sunglasses was standing there, watching the game.

Anton thought the guy looked familiar, but he wasn't Malik's dad. Anton wasn't sure who he was.

The man was pointing toward Malik and jogging in place. It looked like he was pretending to run with the football.

Malik shook his head. Then he turned back to the huddle.

"Okay, guys," he said. "This is it. Last play. Everybody make sure you get your blocks. Give it all you've got on this one!"

All the players nodded. "Yeah, let's win this!" one of them shouted.

Malik stood up straight.

He looked over to the man on the sideline again.

Then he bent back down into the huddle. "Okay, here's the play," he said. "23 fake . . . "

He paused. Then he started over. "No, no," he said. "54 option right. On two."

"What?" Anton yelled. "That's not what the coach called!"

"That play won't work," Malik said. "We're using the 54 option right instead."

"You can't change what the coach says," Anton said. He looked around. The other players seemed nervous.

Malik didn't listen. He started marching up to the line of scrimmage.

Anton knew he had to do something. "Time out!" he yelled to the referee.

CHAPTER 2

A NEW PLAN

Malik and Anton ran to the sideline. Coach Benson looked confused.

"What's going on out there, boys?" the coach asked.

Anton waited to see if Malik was going to tell the coach what happened.

"Coach, I don't think that's the best play for us right now," Malik said. "I think maybe we should run the option. That way, I can make something happen."

"Malik, the play I called has a lot of options to it," Coach Benson said. "The first option is to drop the ball to Anton. If he's covered, you can throw to Jeff downfield."

Malik crossed his arms.

"But Coach," he said, "I know I can do this. Let me run the option, and I'll get us the touchdown we need."

Coach Benson frowned. Anton could tell he was angry.

"Malik, listen to me," the coach said. "We're going to run the play I called. The only way I want you to run with the ball is if everybody is covered. That's your only option."

Then Malik looked the coach right in the eye. "Okay, Coach," Malik said. "We'll do it your way. I got it."

Anton and Malik headed back to the huddle.

On the way back, Anton saw Malik shoot a glance at the tall man on the sideline and give him a little wink.

The tall man waved back at Malik.

Once they reached the huddle, Malik quickly delivered the play call. "Okay, guys, here we go," he said. "It's 23 fake flat right, on two. Everybody make your blocks!"

The team broke the huddle and headed to the scrimmage line.

Malik moved in behind the center and started calling out the signals.

"Down! Set!" he yelled as the players got into position. "Hut! Hut!"

The center snapped the ball.

Malik faked the handoff to Anton, who turned and ran to the right side.

Malik hid the ball from defenders and dropped back into the pocket.

Anton looked back toward Malik, and saw him fake the long pass downfield.

The Dolphin defense was faked out. It worked!

Now Anton was all alone on the right. The play was setting up perfectly.

Malik looked at Anton.

The offensive line was holding off the big Dolphins defenders. Malik had plenty of time.

Malik faced Anton.

He raised his arm, cocked it back, and brought it forward.

Anton got ready to catch the pass.

But Malik didn't release the ball.

Instead, he tucked it under his arm, turned, and headed toward the end zone.

"Yeah, Malik!" the tall man yelled from the sideline. "Go!"

Malik had some room on the left side, but not a lot. He ran the first five yards easily.

Then he faked out two Dolphins defenders and broke free near the 10-yard line.

From there, it was a race to the corner of the end zone.

Anton thought a Dolphins player was about to catch up to Malik. But Malik's speed was too much for him.

He darted into the end zone, raising the ball above his head.

The Giants won. Most of the team ran over to Malik to celebrate.

But Anton stood still.

CHAPTER 3

PLAYING LIKE A TEAM

After the two teams shook hands, all of the Giants players gathered around Coach Benson.

"It's great to start the season with a win, boys," the coach said. "I'm very proud of how hard you worked in this game."

All of the players cheered and gave each other high fives. The coach waited for a few moments to let them celebrate before he continued.

"We do have some things we need to work on, though," Coach Benson said. "It takes time to play like a team. Football is the ultimate team sport, and we'll get better as the season goes along."

Anton thought he knew what Coach Benson meant.

When the coach talked about playing like a team, he was talking about Malik's selfish play at the end of the game.

The more Anton thought about it, he realized the coach was probably right. After all, he and Malik hadn't played together before.

Malik didn't know Anton well enough to know that he could make great plays, too.

So Malik relied on what he did know, which was his own ability.

* * *

By the time the Giants returned to practice the following week, Anton had pretty much forgotten about Malik's play.

When the Giants took the field for the second game of the season, the man in the sunglasses wasn't there.

Anton felt great. He had the feeling they could win the game, if they could play together as a team.

Anton's team was playing against the Jets. The Giants got the ball first.

On the first drive of the game, Malik ran all the plays exactly as the coach had called them.

Anton was surprised and happy to see that the teamwork was really paying off.

Malik handed off to Anton, pitched out to Carlos, passed the ball to Jeff, and the Giants moved the ball down the field with ease.

Finally, the team made it to the Jets' 5-yard line.

Coach Benson called for an option play to the left side.

That meant that Malik would run along the line of scrimmage with the ball.

Anton would trail behind him.

If Malik saw a clear path to the end zone, he'd keep the ball.

If he got in trouble, he was supposed to pitch the ball to Anton.

Anton was worried. What if Malik didn't run the play like he was supposed to?

Here we go again, Anton thought, suddenly feeling worried. He was sure that Malik would decide to keep the ball again on this play.

Malik called out the signals.

When the ball was snapped, Malik ran along the line of scrimmage. Anton was in great position behind him.

As they turned the corner toward the end zone, one of the Jets linebackers approached.

Malik tucked the ball down and turned up field.

Just as the linebacker was about to tackle him, Malik pitched the ball perfectly to Anton.

The linebacker tackled Malik, but the ball was already gone.

Anton had caught it easily.

With no defenders between him and the goal line, Anton cruised into the end zone for a touchdown.

CHAPTER 4

THE MAN IN THE SUNGLASSES

Anton flipped the ball to the referee and ran over to Malik, who was still sitting on the ground.

"Are you all right?" Anton asked.

"Yeah, I'm fine," Malik said. "Man, that guy nailed me. Oh, well. At least we scored a touchdown."

"You played that perfectly," Anton said. "He really thought you were keeping it. I did too."

During the rest of the game, Malik shared the ball with his teammates.

He ran the ball a few times by himself, but only when the coach called for it or when it was Malik's only option.

It was nearly a perfect game.

The Giants ended up winning 35–12.

They had won a game for the second week in a row.

"Boys, we made a lot of improvement this week," Coach Benson said after the game. "Everyone did a great job blocking for each other. We really became a team out there."

After the team meeting, Anton slapped hands with Malik.

"Good game," Anton said.

It seemed like they were becoming friends, and he felt bad about thinking that Malik was a selfish player.

* * *

A week later, the Giants were getting ready to play the Cowboys in their third game of the season.

All of the Giants were on the field, stretching out and warming up.

Malik and Anton were joking around and throwing a football back and forth.

Suddenly, a voice rang out from the other sideline.

"Hey, Malik!" It was the man in the sunglasses.

Malik flipped the ball to Anton and ran over to him.

Malik seemed happy to see the man. The man put his arm around Malik's shoulders. He whispered into Malik's ear, and Malik nodded his head.

After a couple of minutes, Malik ran back to his teammates.

Anton knew the man looked familiar, but he couldn't figure out who the guy was.

He didn't have time to think about it, because the game was about to start.

The Cowboys got the ball first. They moved it quickly down the field and scored a touchdown.

When the Giants got the ball back, they needed to try to score right away.

On their first play, Coach Benson called for the option, which gave Malik a choice.

Malik chose to keep the ball instead of pitching it to Anton. He ran for five yards.

The second play was a running play for Anton, but he was stopped at the line of scrimmage. That made it third down.

Coach Benson called for a pass play.

Malik dropped back to throw the ball. He waited a split second, but instead of throwing the ball, he tucked it down and ran.

He sprinted around the right end, but was stopped short of a first down. The Giants had to punt.

When they came off the field, Coach Benson called Malik over.

"What happened there?" the coach asked. "We had receivers open. Why didn't you throw the ball?"

"I didn't see them," Malik said. He walked away.

In the game against the Jets the week before, Malik had shared the ball. But this game was different.

Malik kept the ball on most of the option plays.

On almost all of the passing plays, he pulled the ball down and tried to run with it.

Still, the Giants scored. Malik was playing selfishly, but he was a good player, so he could get away with it.

With less than a minute to go, the Giants trailed 20–18. Malik had scored all three touchdowns.

With the ball on the Cowboys' 12-yard line, the Giants still had a chance to win.

Coach Benson called for an option play.

As the team jogged up to the line of scrimmage, the man in the sunglasses called out, "Come on, Malik! Win this game! Show them what you can do!"

Suddenly, Anton had a bad feeling in the pit of his stomach.

CHAPTER 5

FAMOUS

Malik took the snap and headed to the right side. The offensive line kept the Cowboys' defensive line under control.

Anton moved into position behind Malik, ready for the pitch.

Malik turned the corner and saw a linebacker, the player he had to beat.

Malik faked a pitchout to Anton, but it didn't fool the linebacker. He kept heading toward Malik.

Still, Malik kept the ball. He tucked it under and tried to fake out the linebacker.

It didn't work.

The linebacker squared his shoulders and wrapped his arms around Malik.

He slammed Malik to the ground.

The ball slid out from Malik's hands and popped free.

Just like that, the Giants' undefeated record was gone. The Cowboys had won the game.

As they jogged off the field, Malik shook his head.

"Why didn't you pitch that to me?" Anton said. "That linebacker was on you."

"I thought I could beat him," Malik said. He shrugged. "I couldn't."

After the game, Coach Benson tried to boost his players' spirits by reminding them of the team's good moments.

Still, Anton could tell that the coach wasn't happy with Malik.

After talking to the team, the coach pulled Malik to the side. He talked to him for a long time.

As Malik walked off the field, the tall man who'd been watching from the sideline headed over to him.

"Great game, Malik!" the man yelled. "Three touchdowns!"

"Yeah, but we lost the game," Anton heard Malik say.

"Don't worry about that," the man said. "You did your part."

Anton couldn't believe what he was hearing.

The man seemed to be telling Malik that his personal statistics were more important than how the team did.

If Coach Benson heard that, Anton knew he wouldn't be happy.

Anton walked home with his teammate Jeff, who played tight end. He told Jeff what he had heard. "Well, that's not too surprising, is it?" Jeff said. "That guy's always been like that."

Anton stopped walking. "You mean you know who that guy is?" he asked.

"Of course," said Jeff. "Don't you?"

Anton shook his head. "I know he looks familiar," he said.

"That's Jerome Biggins. He used to play in the pros," Jeff said.

"Oh! He's the guy who was always doing those crazy touchdown dances and getting fined by the league and stuff, right?" Anton asked.

"Yeah, that's the guy," Jeff said.

"Why does he care about Malik's statistics?" Anton asked, confused.

Jeff stopped and stared at him. "You mean you don't know? Jerome Biggins is Malik's uncle."

CHAPTER 6

TRYING TO LOOK GOOD

Suddenly, Anton understood why Malik was playing selfishly. Malik's uncle was a famous pro football player.

Malik was trying to show off.

But Anton was worried about his team. They had a record of two wins and one loss.

There were only six games left in the regular season. To make it to the playoffs, the Giants had to have at least six wins.

That meant they had to win four of the next six games to qualify.

Malik was a good player. But if he was going to keep playing selfishly, it was going to be tougher for the team to win.

And it might hurt their chances of making it to the playoffs.

Anton wasn't sure how to handle the situation. He didn't want to say anything to Malik, because Jerome Biggins was his uncle.

So Anton decided to talk to Coach Benson.

After the next practice, Anton walked over to the coach. "Coach, can I talk to you for a minute?" he asked.

"Sure," Coach Benson said. "What's up, Anton?"

"I'm worried about Malik, because I think he's trying to show off in front of Jerome Biggins," Anton said.

Coach Benson frowned. "Anton, Malik is a very good player, and he has a lot of confidence," he said. "Sometimes players who have a lot of confidence think they can do everything, and they don't trust their teammates as much. I think as the year goes on, Malik will begin to share the ball more."

Anton decided to trust Coach Benson. But he also started paying more attention to Malik's behavior.

During the two games that Jerome Biggins attended, Malik kept the ball too much. Anton thought it seemed like Malik was showing off during those games.

The Giants lost those two games, but Malik was the team's star both times.

When Jerome wasn't there, Malik played much smarter and shared the ball.

He kept the ball when he should. He pitched it on the option play when he should. And when he dropped back to pass, he threw the ball most of the time.

When Jerome Biggins wasn't there, Malik was a great teammate.

The Giants won both games they played when Biggins did not show up.

With two games remaining, the team had four wins and three losses.

Anton knew they probably needed to win their last two games in order to make the playoffs.

Anton decided that he didn't have a choice. He had to talk to Malik.

Before the next game, Anton pulled Malik aside.

"You're pretty lucky to have an uncle who's a pro football player," Anton said.

Malik smiled.

Anton continued, "I just want to make sure that we're going to play as a team these next two games, like Coach said. We've got to make it to the playoffs. Just because your uncle was a great player doesn't mean you need to show off in front of him."

Malik's smile disappeared. "Show off?" he said. "You think I'm showing off? I'm just playing the game, Anton. I'm just trying to win."

"Yeah? Well, It just seems like when he's here, you don't share the ball as much," Anton replied. "It seems like you're trying to do everything yourself. It seems —"

He stopped when a man approached.

It was Jerome Biggins.

CHAPTER 7

BAD ADVICE

"Hey, Malik. Who's your friend?" Jerome Biggins asked, slapping Malik on the back.

"This is Anton," Malik said. "He's our halfback."

"Cool," Biggins said. He looked at Anton. "You want my autograph?"

Before Anton could respond, Biggins grabbed Anton's helmet out of his hand. Biggins pulled a marker out of his pocket and signed the helmet.

"Here you go, dude," he said. "Enjoy it."

Anton looked at his white helmet, which now had a huge black scrawl on one side. He pretended to be excited. "Um, thanks," he said. He turned to walk away.

Behind him, Biggins started talking to Malik. Anton couldn't help hearing him.

"Listen, Malik, you go out there today and be the man," Biggins said. "Every chance you get, you've got to pull that ball down and run."

"I don't know, Uncle Jerome," Malik replied. "My coach wants me to share the ball. He doesn't like it when I keep it all the time."

Jerome laughed. "You want to be a pro like me, right?" he asked.

"Yeah," Malik said quietly.

"Well, you can't be a pro unless you play college ball," Biggins said. "And you can't play college ball unless you're a star in high school."

"I know," Malik answered. "And I can't be a star in high school unless I make varsity next year, right?"

"Right," his uncle said. He went on, "The varsity coach in this town likes his quarterbacks to be running quarterbacks. They don't pass the ball much. He's always around watching these games, and I want him to see you running the ball, showing your stuff."

Anton was almost to the sideline, where the rest of the team was gathering. He could see the other players drinking water and stretching.

Behind him, Biggins continued, "Malik, you've got a lot of skill," he said. "You've got more talent than I did at your age. You can go all the way if you want to."

"Thanks, Uncle Jerome," Malik said. "I'll think about it."

Suddenly, it became clear to Anton.

Malik hadn't been showing off for his uncle. He'd been following his uncle's instructions.

That day's game was the worst one yet. Malik barely even handed the ball off to Anton when he was supposed to.

He tucked the ball and ran on almost every pass play.

On all the option plays, he kept the ball instead of pitching it to Anton.

Jerome Biggins yelled and cheered for Malik from the sidelines.

Even when Malik got tackled for a loss, Jerome yelled for him to keep the ball the next time.

Fortunately, the Giants were playing against the Rams, the worst team in the league.

The Giants should have beaten the Rams by at least ten points, but they barely managed to win by three.

At least we won, Anton told himself.

Now they had five wins and three losses, with one game left to play.

Their last opponent would be the Dolphins, who were also 5–3 for the season. The winner would go to the playoffs.

But the Giants had a new problem.

Most of the players on the team were mad at Malik for keeping the ball all the time.

Coach Benson was mad too. After the game against the Rams, he pulled Malik aside to talk to him.

Anton heard the coach say angrily, "Listen, young man. We can't have that kind of selfish play. If I can't count on you to share the ball, Malik, maybe I have to find another quarterback."

CHAPTER 8

TURNING IT AROUND

There was only one game left in the season. Anton knew he had to do something.

He felt terrible for Malik. If Coach Benson replaced him and got a new quarterback, the Giants probably wouldn't beat the Dolphins.

Anton also knew that Malik would have to share the ball for the Giants to win.

Anton knew he had to do something.

Anton showed up for the final game of the season ready to have a talk with Malik.

Malik was already at the field. He was standing on the sideline, talking to his uncle.

Anton could hear Biggins talking as he walked up to them.

"The varsity coach is going to be at the game today," Malik's uncle said. "You've got to play your best, man."

"Don't worry, I will," Malik said.

Now Anton was really worried. He was sure that Malik was going to keep the ball for himself for most of the game.

Then the Giants would have no chance of winning the game, and they wouldn't make the playoffs.

The Giants got the ball first, and Coach Benson called for an option play right away.

Sure enough, Malik kept the ball, even though it would have been a better choice to pitch it to Anton.

After Anton carried on the next play, the Giants were faced with third down and five yards to go.

Jeff ran onto the field with the play from Coach Benson. He whispered it to Malik, who turned into the huddle.

"Fifty-four option right, on two," Malik said.

"That's not what Coach Benson said!" Jeff yelled. "He called for a deep pass."

"I don't care," Malik said, shrugging. "This play will work."

The team trotted up to the line.

When Coach Benson saw that the players weren't in the right spots for the play he'd called, he jumped up.

"Time out!" he yelled.

Malik and Anton jogged over to the sideline.

"What's going on out there?" Coach Benson asked. "I called a pass play."

He didn't wait for an answer. "I'm the coach," he said angrily. "When I call the play, I expect it to be run. Are we clear?"

Malik nodded. He and Anton ran back to the huddle.

This time, Malik called the pass play.

When the ball was snapped, Malik dropped back to pass.

Anton ran around the right end and headed out for a pass. Suddenly, Jeff broke free down the sideline.

Malik spotted him and delivered a long pass.

Jeff ran underneath it. He caught the ball in stride and headed straight for the end zone.

None of the Dolphins players had a chance to catch him.

Jeff raised his arms as he crossed the goal line.

As Malik strolled off the field, he glanced toward the varsity coach, who was standing on the sideline.

The coach was clapping his hands. He looked straight at Malik.

"Nice pass!" the varsity coach called. Malik flashed a little smile.

For the rest of the game, Malik was a different player.

He ignored his uncle's yelling. He ran the plays that Coach Benson called. He shared the ball.

He was everything a good quarterback should be.

In the final minutes of the game, the Giants and Dolphins were tied.

With the ball on the Dolphins' 18-yard line, Coach Benson called for the option play.

Malik took the ball down the sideline. He tucked the ball in to draw the linebacker to him, and then pitched the ball to Anton.

The sideline was clear.

Anton cruised in for the winning touchdown.

Anton was thrilled.

The Giants were going to the playoffs!

After the game, Coach Benson gathered the players around him for a talk.

"Congratulations, boys," he said. "That was a real team win. I'm proud of the way you played. Each of you had great moments, but the victory happened because you were playing as a team."

Just then, the varsity coach walked over.

"Boys, I want to introduce you to someone," Coach Benson said. "This is Coach Stevens, the head varsity coach."

All the boys clapped.

Coach Stevens smiled and said, "Boys, that was a great game. I'm looking forward to having you all try out for the varsity team next year. I love to have a team full of hard-working players who want to be great teammates That's how you win games. You all proved that today."

The boys all cheered.

Out of the corner of his eye, Anton noticed that Jerome Biggins was standing alone on the sidelines.

Coach Benson called the boys in closer. "All right, boys," he said. "Let's hear it. On three."

"One, two, three," the boys yelled in unison. "TEAM!"

ABOUT THE AUTHOR

Bob Temple lives in Rosemount, Minnesota, with his wife and three children. He has written more than thirty books for children. Over the years, he has coached more than twenty kids' soccer, basketball, and baseball teams. He also loves visiting classrooms to talk about his writing.

ABOUT THE ILLUSTRATOR

When Sean Tiffany was growing up, he lived on a small island off the coast of Maine. Every day, from sixth grade until he graduated from high school, he had to take a boat to get to school. When Sean isn't working on his art, he works on a multimedia project called "OilCan Drive," which combines music and art. He has a pet cactus named Jim.

GLOSSARY

ability (uh-BIL-i-tee)—skill

approached (uh-PROHCHT)—came up to

autograph (AW-tuh-graf)—someone's signature

confidence (KON-fih-duhnss)—belief in your own abilities

opponent (uh-POH-nuhnt)—someone who is against your team

option (OP-shuhn)—something that you can choose to do. To learn more about the option play, turn to the next page.

pro (PROH)—short for **professional,** a person who makes money for playing sports

scrimmage (SKRIM-ij)—when the two teams line up to face each other, they are on the line of scrimmage

statistics (stuh-TISS-tiks)—a record of how someone has done

ultimate (UHL-tuh-mit)—the best example of something

Many football teams use an offensive system called the "option." The option gets its name because each time it is run, the quarterback (QB) has the option, or choice, to decide what to do with the ball. He can keep it and run it himself, he can hand it to his fullback (FB), or he can pitch it out to his halfback (HB).

As the quarterback gets to the end of his line of blockers, he makes his decision. If there is no defender in his way, he will run with the ball. If he is challenged, he will pitch the ball to his running back.

The play works because the defense doesn't know whether the play is a running or passing play, and who will carry the ball. The option requires a quarterback who is very quick on his feet and can make quick decisions, too.

THE OPTION PLAY

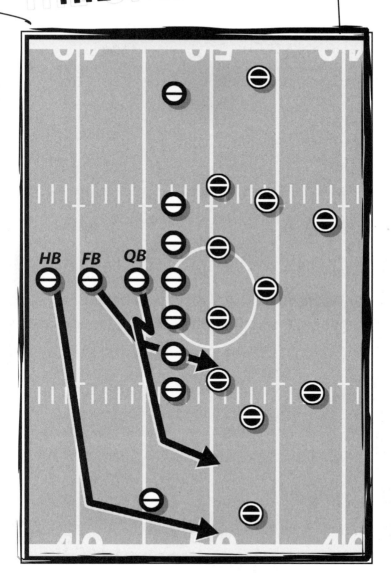

DISCUSSION QUESTIONS

1. Do you think it is more important to help your team win, or to make yourself look good? Talk about which is better.

2. In this book, Malik tries to impress his uncle by doing what his uncle tells him to do. Do you think that was a smart way to behave? What could he have done differently? Talk about Malik's actions.

3. Do you think Anton did the right thing when he talked to his coach about Malik's behavior? Was there something else he could have done?

WRITING PROMPTS

1. How do you think Jerome Biggins felt after the last game in this book? What do you think he might have said to Malik afterward? Write a few paragraphs telling what Malik and Jerome talk about.

2. Who is your favorite pro athlete? Write about the person. Describe how they look and the position they play. What do you like about them? Write about it!

3. Have you ever had to confront a friend or teammate about their actions on the field? What did you say? How was the situation resolved? Write about it.

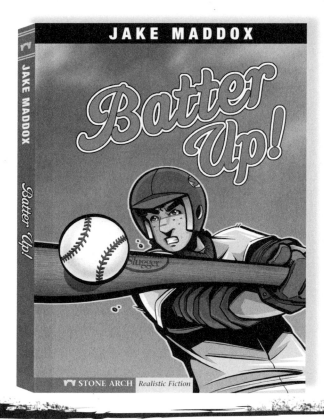

JAKE MADDOX

Batter Up!

STONE ARCH *Realistic Fiction*

Caleb has always batted with the same wood bat — until the other team accuses Caleb of tampering with the bat! Caleb's forced to use the aluminum bat. How is he supposed to help his team win when he keeps striking out?

BY JAKE MADDOX

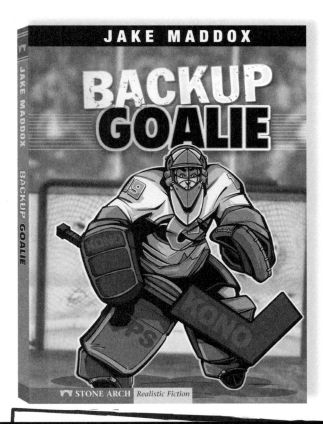

Jamie thought everything was perfect on his hockey team. But when the goalie is injured, Jamie has to step in to the unfamiliar position. Can Jamie help his team skate to victory, or are they on thin ice?

INTERNET SITES

Do you want to know more about subjects related to this book? Or are you interested in learning about other topics? Then check out FactHound, a fun, easy way to find Internet sites.

Our investigative staff has already sniffed out great sites for you!

Here's how to use FactHound:

1. Visit *www.facthound.com*

2. Select your grade level.

3. To learn more about subjects related to this book, type in the book's ISBN number: **9781434204646**.

4. Click the **Fetch It** button.

FactHound will fetch the best Internet sites for you!